SHACKLEBOUND BOOKS

Drabbledark II

First published by Shacklebound Books 2022

Copyright © 2022 by Shacklebound Books

All rights reserved. No part of this publication may be reproduced, stored or transmitted in any form or by any means, electronic, mechanical, photocopying, recording, scanning, or otherwise without written permission from the publisher. It is illegal to copy this book, post it to a website, or distribute it by any other means without permission.

This novel is entirely a work of fiction. The names, characters and incidents portrayed in it are the work of the author's imagination. Any resemblance to actual persons, living or dead, events or localities is entirely coincidental.

First edition

Editing by Eric Fomley

This book was professionally typeset on Reedsy. Find out more at reedsy.com

For Cassy, my better half.

Contents

Introduction	1
A Scorching Mother by Ai Jiang	2
The Mess You've Made by Taylor Rae	3
Inside by Michelle Ann King	4
Beside a Cemetery, a Stone Wall, a Skeletal Tree by Elou Carroll	5
In the Wee Hours by Dorian J. Sinnott	6
Emma by Dorian J. Sinnott	7
After Glow by Liam Hogan	8
By the Coin by Stace Johnson	9
Ephemeral by Antony Frost	10
Playing in the Woods by Carson Winter	11
The Creative Writing Assignment by TJ Price	12
The Scarecrow Sang to Empty Rows of Silage by Mathew Wend	13
Hatman by Chelsea Pumpkins	14
The Quiet Things in Forgotten Spaces by Jessica Peter	16
Cracking Porcelain by Vanessa Jae	17
Light Switch Serenade by Nikki R. Leigh	18
Interior Monologue by John H. Dromey	19
The Drowned Witches of the Ashen Sea by Tea Riffo	20
Post-Apocalyptic Saturday by Patrick Barb	21
Down By The Reef by Grant Butler	22
Cù-Sìth by Emma Louise Gill	23
In the Boneyard Good by Joachim Heijndermans	24
Waiting for a Whisper by Dana Vickerson	25
Mom Swears This Will Work by Tyler Norton	26
The Last Fantasy by Warren Benedetto	27

Everything You Know About Witches by Warren Benedetto	28
Small Mercies by Mob	30
Merdreams by Stephanie Parent	31
Before the Storm by Stephanie Parent	32
Rubin's Vase is Rife With Larvae by Bob McHugh	33
The Hungry by C.M. Saunders	34
Code Blue by NJ Gallegos	35
A Hunger for Company by Kai Delmas	36
Cabbage Dismemberment by Joshua Herz	37
The Bridge Game by Marc Sorondo	38
Knife by Kailey Alessi	39
The Angels by Will Shadbolt	40
The Hunt by Liam Hogan	41
The Outage on Burberry Lane by Dorian J. Sinnott	42
The Horsemen by Cody Simpson	43
The Angel by Warren Benedetto	44
Voices by Kailey Alessi	46
The Wish in the Woods by Abigail Winslow	47
They Came From the Deep by Joe Scipione	48
Life Sentence by M. L. Grieve	49
A Sleeping Sickness by Belicia Rhea	50
The Sommelier by Tess P.	51
Simulation by Andrea Allison	52
Mama by T.L. Beeding	53
Runaway Wood by Ian Kitley	54
Someone to Love by R.A. Goli	55
Trail of Slime by DJ Tyrer	56
A Lidded Black Box by Christopher Wood	57
Got Milk? by Mike Murphy	58
Candle for Knife by Joachim Heijndermans	59
If... by Liam Hogan	60
The Crocodile Promised He'd Eat You Last by Jacob Steven Mohr	61
Siren of the Sand Bar by Dana Vickerson	62

The Count of Three by Cat Voleur	63
What Has Been Given Can Be Taken Away by Stephen Howard	64
The Last Woman by Sarah Jane Huntington	65
The Dance Demon by Renata Pavrey	66
The Trumpet by Will Shadbolt	67
New Life by Clint White	68
The Sounds of Space and Silence by Jenna Hanchey	69
Cŵn Annwn by Ria Rees	70
Payback by Collin Yeoh	71
Surprises Suck by Wondra Vanian	72
Aberrant Foliation by Dennis Mombauer	73
The Coal Ghosts by Abi Marie Palmer	74
Unholy Choir by James Aitchison	75
Torches, Pitchforks by Jacob Steven Mohr	76
Hurricane Warning by Alex Luceli Jiménez	77
Way Up High by Rachel L. Tilley	78
Snow Day by Bethany Browning	79
The Motes by Tess P.	80
Predators and Prey by Taylor Rae	81
Welcome to the Funhouse by Alicia Hilton	82
Publication History	83
Also by Shacklebound Books	89

Introduction

Back in 2018, I discovered drabbles, stories of exactly 100 words. I think it was originally *Trembling With Fear*, a digital market on the Horror Tree website where I saw the form first used. I decided I wanted to try my hand at drabbles, and little did I know how addicting they can really be. I sold several drabbles, but I'd wanted to try my hand at editing for a while and thought of the concept of putting together an anthology of drabbles from various writers. Back in 2018, I hadn't seen anyone else doing drabble anthologies. I didn't know who would even want to write for such an anthology. But I decided to give it a whirl on Kickstarter and was pleasantly surprised when Drabbledark 1 was funded.

I put the call out for genre writers with the only stipulations being that they write a story of exactly 100 words and that the stories be dark. We wound up with 101 morsels of dark science fiction, fantasy, and horror. We discovered together that 100 words are just enough words to creep you out.

So here we are in the beginning pages of Drabbledark 2. We have a bunch more dark science fiction, fantasy, and horror drabbles for your consumption. There are a lot of newer writers in this one, and writers from all over the world. I hope you enjoy what you read, consider looking at some of our other drabble anthologies, and promote the wonderful writers within this volume.

Enjoy the ride.

-Eric Fomley, April 2022

A Scorching Mother by Ai Jiang

Though she keeps us full, she drains us of our living liquids, has us begging to quench our unending thirst, pushes into our bodies what we need for growth, yet takes it all the same. Her harsh rays threaten those who cower under us, delight those who brave the light. Brown, speckle the surfaces of willing humans. Crinkle or strength our hairs, stroking with full beam or, at times, slivers of gold when shielded by moving entities—smoky gods propelled through the sky by the wind. The scorching mother's caress is both a desire and also an enduring pain.

Ai Jiang is a Chinese-Canadian writer, an immigrant from Fujian, and a member of HWA. Twitter (@AiJiang_) and online (http://aijiang.ca).

The Mess You've Made by Taylor Rae

You know the third worst part of a zombie busting through your window? Mopping up the watery brains.

Zombie skulls get soft. All that rot.

The second worst part is when the zombie's your own sister, so you're mopping and crying, mopping and crying. Trying not to notice the necklace suspended from her already-rotting neck. She ragdolls in the window, gutted by glass.

You gave her that necklace. Before the outbreak. Before all this.

But the worst part is coming any second now.

That's when the necklace twitches. You realize your sister isn't dead. Not yet.

But she is hungry.

Taylor Rae's work has appeared with *Flash Fiction Online, NYC Midnight,* and *Pseudopod*. For more, check out www.mostlytaylor.com

Inside by Michelle Ann King

'Hi, darling,' said the thing that looked like my husband.

It was amazingly good, to be fair. A perfect duplicate. I should probably be flattered at the effort involved.

Then again, there could be hundreds of them out there. Most people don't pay attention the way I do.

'Coffee?' it said, handing me a mug that undoubtedly had some kind of drug inside. They had to know I was suspicious.

What was inside that body, I wondered? Cogs and wires, dirt and clay, green blood and unrecognisable, alien organs?

I selected a knife from the drawer. Time to find out.

Michelle Ann King writes speculative, crime, and horror fiction that has appeared in over a hundred different magazines and anthologies.

Beside a Cemetery, a Stone Wall, a Skeletal Tree by Elou Carroll

Beneath frost hard as teeth, the bone tree reaches out its gnarled fingers. It tipsteps atop the stone wall — waits — and snatches a crow from her perch.

Back in the tree's trunk, it strips the bird of flesh and feathers. The domed skull and sternum are added to the skeletal ephemera of its roots, dug deep in the frigid earth. A breeze passes, stale like breath, and the osseous branches rattle.

Another crow lands alone on the wall and caws long and loud, lowers his head, and lingers there. He calls for his mate, but only the bone tree answers.

Elou Carroll likes to tell ghost stories. She tweets from @keychild. You can find her work on www.eloucarroll.com.

In the Wee Hours by Dorian J. Sinnott

I could hear her scuttling across the attic floor, dragging her limp body as she moaned. Each and every night I would stay awake, pleading that my father not turn out the light. Fearful of what awaited in the shadows.

If *she* ever made it out.

But he assured me that it was just my mind. Wild imagination playing tricks in the wee hours of night. And so he went to bed, forgetting to lock the attic door...

Across the room, I could see her in the doorway. Mouth wide and neck crooked as she moaned. Clambering towards my bed.

Dorian J. Sinnott's work has appeared in over 190 journals and has been nominated for the Best of the Net.

Emma by Dorian J. Sinnott

It was after the blizzard that Robert heard it—calling from the wood. The voice of his Emma, whispering his name on the winter wind. It had been so sweet, just as he always knew. Honeyed. Full of love. But still, he kept his rifle close, eyes fixed on the window that overlooked the dense forest. Telling himself not to listen. Not to give in. No matter how she beckoned him. No matter how much he loved her…

The truth hurt.

For it couldn't have been his beloved Emma. He had buried her that prior spring. Out amongst the trees.

Dorian J. Sinnott's work has appeared in over 190 journals and has been nominated for the Best of the Net.

After Glow by Liam Hogan

Huh. Zombies.

Of course it was zombies. The apocalypse scenario that never dies. The dead reborn through the years. Fast zombies, slow zombies, space zombies. Explained away by genetically engineered viruses, or airborne fungal spores, or alien parasites. All of them after your flesh, if not your brains.

A numbers game; the dead quickly overpowering the living and, after a bite or two, converting hunted to hunter.

There shouldn't be enough nourishment to keep them all going. Didn't make sense.

But, as Malcolm smashed through the rotten skull with his Louisville slugger, at least *these* zombies glow in the dark.

Liam Hogan is an award-winning short story writer, published by *Analog, Daily Science Fiction,* and *Flame Tree Press.* http://happyendingnotguaranteed.blogspot.co.uk

By the Coin by Stace Johnson

I come to you again unbidden, unwelcome, inevitable. As I foretold centuries ago, your leaders have lured you astray. Peace flees from your hearts, and your children die as men on crimson battlefields. The land you loved is war-spoiled, and the sky you worshiped roils with dragon breath.

I hold the end to your strife; I offer it to you, freely. But you are ruled by the coin, and will remain naught more than petty fools.

So light the pyre. I shall be reborn, in yet another dark age, and find you in shallow graves with silver on your eyes.

Stace Johnson is a writer, poet, and musician in Colorado. He has published drabbles previously with *Martian Magazine*.

Ephemeral by Antony Frost

I've been seeing something lately; an ephemeral presence performing a quivering dance at
  the edge of my vision.
  Walking to work, I'm blinking away rain and bitter wind.
  The presence follows; dancing, taunting.
  The route follows the main road. Cars drive past, lights still on in the early morning gloom.
  The presence vies for my attention. It fills my ears with static.
  I ignore it.
  The ephemeral shapes encroach further. They become cascading forms of light and
  shadow, obscuring everything.
  I stagger, stumble. Did I step off the footpath?
  I hear a car horn.
  But I can't see the car.

Antony Frost is a podcaster and author of horror and weird fiction from Cambridgeshire, UK. More from him at linktr.ee/AntonyFrost

Playing in the Woods by Carson Winter

There is an old house in the woods, made of oak and stone. A furnace purrs from inside, white smoke pours from the chimney.

"Whatever happens will be beautiful," she says.

"You promise?"

"Would I ever lie to you?"

She goes in first, disappearing through the doorway. He waits and listens for her.

He hears the loud clanging of an iron door being shut. There is a pop and stutter—the sound of bacon frying in the morning.

The smoke is black and inky. He hears her.

"*Go ahead, come in,*" she says.

He steps into the blackness, to join her.

Carson Winter is an author, punker, and raw nerve. His work has been published in *Vastarien: A Literary Journal*, *Apex Magazine*, and *The No Sleep Podcast*. He lives in the Pacific Northwest.

The Creative Writing Assignment by TJ Price

Write 100 words about what "home" means to you.

The paper's face is as barren as a clock's. I can hear my eyes ticking in my skull.

All around me, the secretive sibilance of words, pouring out of my classmates' pencils, no doubt describing

Warm kitchens.

Smiles so big they bruise.

Nuzzles at bedtime.

~~Home is a place the dark isn't supposed to get into but it does anyway~~

Home is where, every night, I hear the sound of Mother's hurried footsteps, then the snap of windows, locking, and I lay there in the dark, thinking about things that shatter...

TJ Price's poltergeist can be found on Twitter @eerieyore; his other ghosts are in Coffin Bell Journal and Complete Sentence.

The Scarecrow Sang to Empty Rows of Silage by Mathew Wend

We buried bones to build our garden, ocher stalks against a graven sky. When the devilish ravens flew by, when the meat never sprouted, when the fallow struck our bellies and all we ate was dirt and muck and measly little things we chose to never mention, that's when the Man in the Chair came.

"Please sit," he purred, "I'll make it alright," and we listened and sat because what else was there to do? "When my work's done, you'll be just right."

And we were, in a way, when all was done and our bones helped feed the sky.

Mathew can be found on twitter @matwend, at the library suggesting horror, and with his wife Bailey and dog Arrow.

Hatman by Chelsea Pumpkins

I met The Hatman in my bedroom, I knew it was a dream.
   The darkness of his void stripped me down.
   Just a dream, just a dream.
   He'd come again from time to time,
   lurk in the shadows of the windowblinds,
   and wait.

* * *

I saw The Hatman in the shower, I knew something was wrong.
   It's not a dream, I'm not asleep.
   It's not where he belongs.
   Steam cascades around his silhouette, water dripping from his brim,
   and in a breath he's gone. And I'm left
   waiting.

* * *

I found The Hatman in the mirror, but now he has my eyes.

Chelsea Pumpkins feeds her life-long hunger for horror by way of dark literature and film. Follow Twitter and Instagram @ChelseaPumpkins.

The Quiet Things in Forgotten Spaces by Jessica Peter

"Visitor." My own voice echoes through the farmhouse. "Visitor. Visitor."

Cooper's not in his spot at the end of the bed. Evidently, he's in the den, pushing one of the buttons I programmed for him.

"Coop, what is it bud?"

No click-clack of nails. I drag myself out of bed, cold feet on the bare floor.

"Visitor. Visitor."

I round the corner. Cooper stands there, one paw on a button as he stares down a shadowed corner. An empty corner. Or is it?

For a moment I see a figure.

But then I flick on the lights, and we're alone.

Jessica Peter is a writer from Hamilton, Ontario, Canada. You can find her on Twitter @jessicapeter1 or at www.jessicapeter.net.

Cracking Porcelain by Vanessa Jae

She marched through town square every night, the hem of her long pink dress drenched in dirty water. The heels of her battered boots composed a melody on the cobblestone, the sound echoing through the silent homes lining the streets. It became the ballad of the children's nightmares, a lullaby seeping deep into the marrow of their bones. Her doll face was illuminated by the full moon, frozen into a grimace it reflected in the empty windows she knew the parents were cowering behind, listening to her ritual and their brood scratching at the floorboards their bedrooms were barricaded with.

Vanessa Jae writes horrifically beautiful anarchies, reads stories for *Apex Magazine* and translates for Progressive International.

Light Switch Serenade by Nikki R. Leigh

The lights dim.

Too dark to see the four of us huddled in the living room, soaked from the rain. Driven in from the fields we were playing in. The noise…God, that noise.

The lights raise.

There we are, shivering. Scared. At a loss for what shook the earth and sent us scattering.

My chest tightens when my gaze lands on the shape. Something in the corner—someone.

The lights dim.

The sound of clothes hitting the floor fills the room. Not, clothes. Something…wetter.

The lights raise. The skinless thing attacks. Noises, just as awful as before.

My vision dims.

Nikki R. Leigh is a queer forever-90s-kid wallowing in all things horror. Find her on Twitter @fivexxfive and Instagram @spinetinglers.

Interior Monologue by John H. Dromey

Hosting an invasive extraterrestrial organism is a daunting task. That's especially true when interplanetary travel is involved.

Astronauts can collect alien specimens with relative ease, but viability is a challenge. Physiologies differ greatly.

Some individuals enjoy an adrenaline rush. Others do not.

Our ability to secrete endorphins at will gives us a distinct advantage. Judiciously released, we can keep a host organism relatively calm until we suck the life out of it.

For instance, human beings—a local, generic term for the dominant species—are surprisingly receptive, provided we can fool them into thinking our relationship with them is symbiotic.

John H. Dromey enjoys reading—mysteries in particular—and writing in a variety of genres.

The Drowned Witches of the Ashen Sea by Tea Riffo

Long fingers extrude from the sea, dark fingernails wrinkling as they crook, beckoning me forward. Somewhere between my ears, the women beneath the water's surface are whispering their enticing incantation.

Come, Play.

Slipping into the water's cool and soft embrace, my teeth shake against frigid waves. The darkness of the womens' magic rushes through my veins, enchanting my skin into the same greyed tone of the hand, which drowns once more.

Come. Play.

I submerge myself completely in the water. Salt, ash, and ocean fill my throat as I join the coven of dead witches scattered across the ocean floor.

Tea Riffo is a poet and essayist who loves witches and plants. Follow her daily writing on twitter at @soteariffic.

Post-Apocalyptic Saturday by Patrick Barb

On this post-apocalyptic Saturday morning, smoke's in the air and murder-focused crows scratch at the last dead-end street, pecking at potholes.

Children with gasmask-covered faces run free (but never *carefree*, not anymore), breaking up flickering holographic propaganda images of the Bloated Men.

Our new, swollen rulers, pickled in hate, tell us, "It's all your fault."

But they're hiding from the poison deluge in faraway lands—insisting in the validity of the American dream.

Isn't it great?

Sounds like freedom. "Remember that chart-topping ditty?"

Then, they play it for us. Over and over, again and again, until we forget the rest.

Patrick Barb is an author whose fiction appears in a variety of recognized horror and speculative fiction venues. Visit patrickbarb.com.

Down By The Reef by Grant Butler

I've known about my wife and my brother Mike for a while, but I never said anything before we all went out on my boat. Since they wanted to be together without me and love getting a thrill, I gave them what they wanted. So when they went snorkeling down by the reef, I pulled up anchor and started the boat back to shore. So they get to be alone 100 miles out to sea. Although they're not completely alone if you count the sharks out there. Between the hammerheads and the great whites, they will have plenty of company.

Grant Butler is the author of the novel *The Heroin Heiress* and his short fiction has been published in *Sick Cruising* and *Mardi Gras Mysteries*.

Cù-Sìth by Emma Louise Gill

Step off the blood-slick rain stones. Run to the dead-hair moors with me. Can't tell you the time nor the year, so don't ask. What does it matter to such as I?

Moonlight stains all in blanching shadows. Gray is the night and the dawn without sun. Is this the afterlife? I cannot say. Just drag you along, drag you down

    down

    down

    down.

Away from the city, the knife, the howls. Beneath the burnt peat to my Undermoor. There, Myth and Death collide.

In that dark I will gather your soul.

In this dark you will feed my children.

Emma Louise Gill (she/her) is a British-Australian speculative fiction writer, dreamer, and coffee addict. She blogs at www.emmalouisegill.com.

In the Boneyard Good by Joachim Heijndermans

Mem hid me in the boneyard good when fireborn won. No more knights or folks. Just fireborn.

Mem say: "Hide in the boneyard good. Never let them find you. Mem will come back." Then she ran to find brother, who'm out warrin'. She left me lone in the boneyard good.

I wait'm an' hid as told. Quiet an' small in day. Quieter an' smaller when fireborn flew past. There, in the boneyard good, I wait'm for Mem. They never find me. Not even when I grew tall an' get Mem's long hair.

I still keep wait in the boneyard good.

Joachim Heijndermans is a writer and artist from the Netherlands. His work is featured in SFFH magazines, podcasts, and animation.

Waiting for a Whisper by Dana Vickerson

Why have you not come, my dark one, my lovely tormentor? Am I to sit in this rotten, dismal cabin until dawn?

I did not mean to betray you.

The wax candles burn low, and you have never taken this long to appear. You always come to me upon the first creeping tendrils of nightfall on our long standing annual appointment. You steal the light away, and in total darkness you bring me a name. The one I am to erase.

Please don't forsake me. Last year was a mistake. Please, my dark one, I will not fail you again.

Dana's work appears in *Trembling with Fear* and Tales to Terrify and upcoming in *Human Monsters*. She's on Twitter @dmvickerson.

Mom Swears This Will Work by Tyler Norton

"Do you remember the prayer I taught you?" Mom asks before opening the door.

I nod. She says this will make Daddy better.

He's been sick for a long time. I miss playing hide and seek, and I miss when he makes waffles for breakfast. He doesn't leave his room anymore.

Mom says I need to be brave for Daddy. I say I will. Then she pushes me inside and slams the door.

The room smells like the dirty dishwasher. It's dark, but I can see his red eyes and yellow teeth.

"Cassie, sweetie, come and give Daddy a hug!"

Tyler Norton's work has previously appeared in *The Arcanist*, *The Final Girl Bulletin Board*, and Ghost Orchid Press' *Home* anthology.

The Last Fantasy by Warren Benedetto

UPLOAD COMPLETE.

Simon disconnected the cable from his patient's skull, checked she was still unconscious, then turned to his screen. He navigated through the mind drive, bypassing memories, diving deeper, through the subconscious, past fears and shame, to his destination: fantasy.

The patient was beautiful. She surely harbored secret desires that would gratify Simon's voyeurism. Simon selected her last fantasy, then watched it play on screen:

The woman's eyes open.
She sees Simon.
Smiles.
Draws a blade.
Slits his throat.

Horrified by the violent images, Simon looked down at his patient.

Her eyes opened.

She smiled, then drew her blade.

Warren Benedetto writes short fiction about horrible people doing horrible things. Visit www.warrenbenedetto.com and follow @warrenbenedetto on Twitter.

Everything You Know About Witches by Warren Benedetto

"Everything you think you know about witches is wrong," Selena sobbed. She struggled against the ropes binding her to the pole.

Father Hugo stuffed kindling under the logs at her feet. He cocked an eyebrow skeptically. "Everything?"

"Everything," Selena insisted.

"Brewing potions?"

"Wrong."

"Casting spells?"

"Wrong!"

Father Hugo lit a match.

"Shapeshifting?"

Suddenly, Selena's face elongated into a long black beak. Feathers sprouted as massive wings unfolded from her back.

Her raven form lunged, driving her beak straight through Father Hugo's face.

As Selena returned to her human shape, she wiped the blood from her mouth.

"Okay, maybe not *everything*."

Warren Benedetto writes short fiction about horrible people doing horrible things. Visit www.warrenbenedetto.com and follow @warrenbenedetto on Twitter.

Small Mercies by Mob

Your clouded eyes never saw the Firstborn.

When the blackened sun twisted in a red sky and we slipped through, you only felt us—chilled skin and a burning gut. Something missing that you'd never put to words. You heard the screams though.

Hard not to.

Fled with the rest, though they didn't keep you long. Dead weight. No use for toys in a wasteland.

But we loved you as you crawled for miles. Through wire. Dust. Into our jaws. *Innocence.* How fresh.

Shhhh, don't cry. It could be worse.

Just listen to the others. You could be so much worse.

Mob writes, when they aren't bouldering or coding. They also run a weekly feature and writing group on Reddit's /r/WritingHub.

Merdreams by Stephanie Parent

Salt thickened her blood; the ocean filled her veins. Whenever her skin broke open, the wound stung from the inside out. Briny crystals lingered on her tongue, pooled at the corners of her eyes. She didn't belong with thin-blooded, dry-eyed humans. The ocean pulled her, a hook stabbing her tender belly. She was a fish on a line, drawn toward water rather than land. The waves would welcome her, recognize the salt inside her and alchemize her lungs.

When the salt water stopped up her throat and her body gasped for oxygen, the betrayal was its own kind of death.

Stephanie Parent is a graduate of the Master of Professional Writing program at USC.

Before the Storm by Stephanie Parent

The children paraded around the parking lot, Spidermen and Wonder Women ready to save the day. In the woods beyond the school, eyes peered from the shadows. Human eyes that wore a costume every day—a costume of shirt and jeans, a costume that said *I'm one of you*.

The children flung candy wrappers shiny as the stars that would watch them, after darkness fell, when they called out "Trick-or-Treat."

In the woods, a tongue darted and licked.

The children shivered as if a cold breeze had flown by. Still the sun shone; there was no sign of a storm.

Stephanie Parent is a graduate of the Master of Professional Writing program at USC.

Rubin's Vase is Rife With Larvae by Bob McHugh

I ran my fingers through Jeremy's curly hair and pointed at the optical illusion. "Girl or witch?"

"Old hag," Jeremy said.

"I only see the young woman."

"Her necklace is the witch's mouth."

"Aha! Now I can't see the girl," I laughed.

I reached for his hair and shrieked; bloody maggots writhed around his scalp.

"Wait, do you see the grubs?" he asked. "No one ever has."

I nodded.

"Thank God. I thought I was crazy. How do I see my hair?"

I wanted to help him, but his locks were gone. They would always be maggots to me now.

Bob McHugh is a Boston-based writer and father of two; he is immensely grateful to be both of those things.

The Hungry by C.M. Saunders

We'd set sail in fair weather. It had all seemed so glorious then. Thirty-three men, all with a shared goal. But things turned sour. Storms, disease. Tragedy followed tragedy, almost as if the ship was jinxed. Weeks turned into months. The food ran out, and the men turned on each other. The weak were slaughtered and their meat used to sustain the strong. There's but a handful left now, and they are hungry. I barricaded myself in my quarters where I sat and prayed to be forgotten about. But my prayers went unanswered. I can hear them at the door.

Christian Saunders, who writes fiction as C.M. Saunders, is a writer and editor from south Wales. His fiction has appeared in almost 100 magazines, ezines and anthologies worldwide and his books have been both traditionally and independently published, the latest release being X5, his fifth volume of short fiction.

https://cmsaunders.wordpress.com/

https://twitter.com/CMSaunders01

https://www.facebook.com/CMSaunders01

Code Blue by NJ Gallegos

"Code Blue" echoes overhead. I race to the elevator—destination ICU. The doors *whoosh* closed, and a jolt shakes me off balance—*damn thing's stuck.* Overhead lights flicker then extinguish. Oppressive darkness encloses me, wrapping its arms around me like a deadly nursemaid. My heart gallops and adrenaline mainlines into my system. *Stay calm, just chill, soon it'll be working again.* Still… my breath quickens, my blind eyes roam, searching for light, for solace—none in sight. My rational mind whispers, *"You're just fine."* A glacial caress traces my cheek; a death rattle intonation, "Doctor, why didn't you save me?"

NJ Gallegos is an Emergency Physician who delights in writing macabre fiction. She does not like hospital elevators.

A Hunger for Company by Kai Delmas

Consciousness used to be fleeting. Singular emotions set free by visitors seeped into my stonework and hardwood floors.

They read my books, satiating me for centuries. Keeping me dormant. Satisfied.

Times have changed.

No one wanders my halls anymore. My bookshelves are covered in dust, worn spines of countless books remain untouched and I wait. Lonely. Hungry.

And I dream.

I dream of company.

Of joy and laughter as visitors read my books.

Of their boots treading on my salivating carpets, ready to strike.

Of fear as they realize my doors are shut and they have no place to run.

Kai loves creating worlds and magic systems. His fiction is forthcoming in *Martian* and *Tree and Stone*.

His Twitter @KaiDelmas

Cabbage Dismemberment by Joshua Herz

The cabbages on Farmer Dave's land are exhausted from growing nonstop. One season, no cabbages grow. In his anger, Dave starts ripping out crops, killing his cabbages.

As Dave reaches down to pull out the next unlucky plant, a root darts out of the ground, grabbing onto Dave's hands. Despite his thrashing and screaming, Dave is relentlessly dragged underground. His limbs are ripped apart by red and green cabbage alike.

However, with no farmer and no common goal, infighting between the red and green cabbage varieties gradually ensues. In the end, both the cabbages and Dave return to the dirt.

Joshua Herz is an author from San Diego, California. He enjoys writing and playing with his dog, Iroh.

The Bridge Game by Marc Sorondo

"I'm tired of this game," Edward said just a few days after his thirteenth birthday. They'd played the game for years, running over the bridge after dark, tempting the troll that lived among the cold, dank stones beneath, proving their bravery.

"It's not like there's really a troll down there," he added, condescension in his tone.

George, still twelve but barely, answered, "Says you. Go down beneath if you're so brave."

Just like that the terms of the game had changed. Edward went beneath the bridge to prove his bravery. He went alone.

None of us ever saw him again.

Marc Sorondo lives with his wife and children. He's a perpetual student and occasional teacher. Check out MarcSorondo.com.

Knife by Kailey Alessi

I always knew how I would die. At five years old, I told my mother that I was bleeding.

"Where?" she asked.

"I don't know," I said. "But I'm bleeding." Mother looked me over and didn't find a single scratch.

"You're completely fine. Don't scare me like that," she said.

So I didn't.

I learned to keep my visions to myself. Ignored the sharp pain that stabbed right between my ribs, the ghostly knife puncturing my lung.

It's almost a relief to be here, lying on the ground, blood gushing from my chest, breaths gasping. The knife has finally arrived.

Kailey Alessi has lived in Michigan and Idaho. An anthropology graduate student by day, by night she writes disturbing fiction.

The Angels by Will Shadbolt

The wings arrived in April. Flaps of skin with two white, feathery wings shooting out. They came for people, flew them high into the heavens. Jones watched the news awe-struck.

"I've been chosen," those with wings would shout. It was an honor. It had to be. Evidence the divine picked them.

One came for Jones. It fused to his back, took him into the clouds. Only then did he realize the truth.

Nothing angelic about them.

These were parasites, taking their prey to where they could get no help. And in May, the first few chosen fell back to earth.

Will Shadbolt works in publishing and lives in Connecticut. You can read more at willshadbolt.com and on Twitter at @W_Shadbolt.

The Hunt by Liam Hogan

We followed the blackened feathers. From the bowl-shaped crater filled by the stench of char, the trail meandered ever downwards, through twisted ravines and eternally dark gorges. The icy stream we traced was swallowed by the gaping maw of a cave. We lit torches and forged on.

The hunt came to an end deep underground. At first we did not realise we had found our quarry; a tattered, unmoving, foul smelling mass. Eyes that had seen God watched without fear from a blood-drenched, soot-blackened face as we raised spears and axes.

To offer them, prostrating ourselves before our dark Lord.

Liam Hogan is an award-winning short story writer, published by *Analog, Daily Science Fiction,* and *Flame Tree Press.* http://happyendingnotguaranteed.blogspot.co.uk

The Outage on Burberry Lane by Dorian J. Sinnott

It was 4:53pm when the residents of Burberry Lane met in the street. They complained about power outages—strange surges—except Sally, who couldn't get their attention. She moved her hands to sign out words, asking what was wrong, but no one noticed her.

They only stopped when a transformer at the end of the block blew. And then another. Up and down the street.

Then came the high-pitched squeal, hissing from sparking wires. They covered their ears, brains rattling until they burst. As their bodies hit the pavement, blood seeping from their ears, Sally could only watch in shock.

Dorian J. Sinnott's work has appeared in over 190 journals and has been nominated for the Best of the Net.

The Horsemen by Cody Simpson

Distant footfalls echoed. The pair huddled for warmth, or fear. Shattered frames, void of their contents sat encased in ash, reminders of the past. Hoofbeats joined the haunting orchestra outside. The mother's hand grasped her daughter's tightly, her delicate whimpers breaking their fortitude.

The sun would soon relinquish its right to the sky, enveloping them in a stale darkness they would never escape.

Still the Horsemen came. The reeking scent of decay announced their arrival. Terrifying screeches raised the mother's flesh. They could hide no longer. In a moment, it was over.

Even after death, their intertwined hands held firm.

Cody Simpson has found a love of writing and between parenting and working he still strives to achieve his goals.

The Angel by Warren Benedetto

"Want some, Daddy?"

Jeff's daughter held the can out to him. It was their last.

"No, baby. You finish."

The girl spooned another peach into her mouth. Dribbles of sweet juice cut clean streaks

down her filthy chin.

"Daddy?"

"Yes?"

"Will you be sad when I die?"

"No."

"Why not?"

Jeff glanced at the festering black bite mark on her arm. The infection was spreading.

"Because you'll come back," he said.

"Like Mommy did? As a monster?"

"Not a monster. An angel."

"And you'll still love me?"

Jeff nodded, then tightened his grip on the gun in his pocket.

"Always."

Warren Benedetto writes short fiction about horrible people doing horrible things. Visit www.warrenbenedetto.com and follow @warrenbenedetto on

Twitter.

Voices by Kailey Alessi

The boy covered his ears, wincing.

They were too loud, all of them yelling at him. And he couldn't understand them, their words were too staticky.

He opened his eyes to see his father crouched in front of him, face understanding. Gently, he pulled the boy's hands away from his ears.

"I know it's loud," he said, "but you'll be able to block them out eventually. You did good for your first time."

The boy took his father's offered hand. Once they left the graveyard, he let out a sigh of relief. The voices of the dead had finally quieted.

Kailey Alessi has lived in Michigan and Idaho. An anthropology graduate student by day, by night she writes disturbing fiction.

The Wish in the Woods by Abigail Winslow

A chrysanthemum flourished amidst the desolate forest. Soft petals, devoid of imperfection, lit up the night.

She plucked the once-mythical flower, tightly gripping her last hope to leave this spellbound darkness. Elation collapsed into fear as the petals disintegrated into ash that flaked through her palms.

Her pale fingertips gave way as vines and bark shrouded them. Joints crackled and stiffened to the spot she stood. Cries of the anguished souls, victims who believed in the lore, echoed as she joined the dense thicket. The forest fell silent, and the tree watched in horror as the flower bloomed once again.

Abigail Winslow is a work by day, write by night author. You can find her other short stories on Amazon.

They Came From the Deep by Joe Scipione

Upon the cliff he stood, watching the coastline. Waves crashed into rocks, against sand. Wind blew sand in his face, stinging his cheeks. Above, the sun shone down doing nothing to warm him.

"There's nothing I can do," he said. "They'll come and end us all."

From between the waves, bodies emerged out of the surf. They were massive creatures, featureless monsters with flat, dull eyes. They resembled fish more than humans but had hands and feet and claws. The beach was covered with hundreds of them—thousands. They looked up at him and roared in unison.

"We are finished."

Joe Scipione is the author of *Perhaps She Will Die* and *Zoo: Eight Tales of Animal Horror*.

Life Sentence by M. L. Grieve

I saw her last night, wretched, bedraggled, and vengeful. Today, a weeping sky mirrored the lamentation of my futile remorse.

Parked at the cemetery, her resting place, I now knew peace eluded us both. This was on me.

Contemplating the bulging grave adorned with my rotting, scarlet gerberas, I turn on the engine to warm my freezing conscience.

Only one week in the ground and she was back.

Drip…Is the car leaking?

I turn to see rainwater gathering in the indented seat. A death-stench descends, as the icy breath of hateful vengeance penetrates my ear.

"I have come for you."

M. L. Grieve is a writer of dark poetry and prose. All her first drafts are written in ancient forests.

Twitter @page_soul

A Sleeping Sickness by Belicia Rhea

The shadowy figure at the foot of the bed grips my legs. My tongue lies dead in my mouth. Breathing fights each bone of my rib cage. A leaky faucet is still dripping, louder, closer, or maybe that's inside my head. What is that? I feel the wet, now pattering against my thighs. Blood trickles from its claws as its scarlet smeared mouth curls into a growl, fangs glistening. The figure drags long nails across my skin, up to my shoulders, holds them down. My arms and legs are stone. Those haunted eyes meet mine and watch me, tonight's prisoner.

Belicia Rhea writes dark fiction and poetry, appearing in *Nightmare Magazine*, among other places. You can find her at beliciarhea.com.

The Sommelier by Tess P.

Sensual, tannin sips and champagne compliments had lured her to this chasmic well, of no return. His intoxicating promises of care and understanding were lip service lies, so sweetly decanted, that she had savoured each delicious drop. Strapped in the cellar, she wondered how many missing women were fermenting within these barrels of oak, drunken dreams. What vintage would she become? 2022: 'A complex, elegant wine, composed of gullible grapes with inviting aromas of innocent vanilla, playful plum, and naïve fig. Full-bodied. Best served chilled.' He licked his cracked lips, corkscrew in gloved hand, one gleaming glass.

"Bienvenue," he whispered.

Tess pens horror shorts and dark drabbles. You'll find her on Twitter @Tess_2020 engaging within the writing community.

Simulation by Andrea Allison

"Help me up, Zoe. Zoe?"

"Sorry Jack." Flames crept up his body as she closed the door, sealing it tight. "Kate!"

"Yes ma'am?"

"Get the boys to set up another simulation by Friday. Find new beta testers. Smarter ones this time. The client wants his puzzle rooms operational by the end of the month."

"What about the bodies, ma'am?"

"Call Mr. Latham. He knows what to do. Transcribe my notes while I'm being stitched up in the infirmary. The biker bar room was too easy to figure out. Maybe add an acid element. We have to get this right, Kate."

Andrea Allison's work has appeared in *Trembling With Fear* and *NoSleep Podcast*. See more at www.andreallison.com.

Mama by T.L. Beeding

It'd been 5 days since Bethany went missing.

John and I searched everywhere she could be. The basement, her closet, school. We even travelled to the neighbors, desperate for answers; but no one had any.

That was, until Lisa told us about the "witch's cottage" they'd found in the woods.

We descended through the trees like wildfire, searching every brush and branch. Following Lisa's childish directions. Eventually we found the clearing she described, but no cottage and no Bethany. Just a rotting baby doll wearing a blue dress and white shoes - like Bethany's.

"Mama," it whined, eyes rolling toward us.

T.L. Beeding is co-editor of *Crow's Feet Journal* and *Paramour Ink*. She can be found on Twitter at @tlbeeding, and at her website, tlbeeding.com.

Runaway Wood by Ian Kitley

These young fools run from their broken homes. Down into bleach-white forest, shirts catching, pants tearing on barren limbs. When they trip, they're blind to roots slithering across the path, as blood drips from scraped knees, sacrificed to thirsty earth.

Scrambling, they ignore terrified visages within the bark, believing darkness deceives, doomed to the same fates as runaways past. When they fall victim to my forest of graves, they realise their mistake. All things hunger, and must be fed, and my wood prefers a compost of living flesh. Thus entombed beneath the dirt, where only trees will hear them scream.

Ian Kitley writes the weird and wonderful in the world of now. Join him and others at https://twitter.com/TheInkwellWC

Someone to Love by R.A. Goli

Berick swore it wasn't because she was barren when he left. Though he'd impregnated his new wife within months. Now Luna was handing over a pouch – heavy with coin – to a brown-toothed old witch.

They walked past crates of little limbs and torsos. Tiny organs sat in jars - lungs, hearts, brains – full of a sickeningly pink, viscous fluid.

Luna lifted the sleeping babe from the crib, bringing him to her chest. Crude stitching lined his neck and wrists. His clothing hid more scars beneath.

He would never leave her; would always be dependent.

Because he would never grow up.

R.A. Goli is an Australian writer of horror and fantasy.

Check out her collection of short stories, *Unfettered*, at https://ragoliauthor.wordpress.com/

Trail of Slime by DJ Tyrer

In those rare harsh winters, when snow falls on Dōgo Island, Tendokumushi leaves its lair, trailing yellow slime that melts the snow.

Big and black, slug-like, suppurating, those who see it recoil in disgust, leaving it alone.

A certain sage, who did not fear or loathe, approached Tendokumushi. Upon its back, he saw a sign: The character for 'heaven'.

"How wonderful!" he declared. "This creature might lead the way to enlightenment."

And, he commenced to follow the trail of slime.

But, its slime also melted ice and, as the sage followed it across a frozen stream, his quest abruptly ended.

DJ Tyrer is the person behind *Atlantean Publishing* and you can find out about their writing by visiting https://djtyrer.blogspot.co.uk/

A Lidded Black Box by Christopher Wood

Dawn mist rolled in off the Loch. Brochan walked the beach, picking tourists' half-buried detritus from the sands. A lidded black box lay washed ashore, caught among jagged rocks of a tide pool. Muffled scratching emanated from within. Casting an eye to the other volunteers, he lifted the lid. Hollow darkness engulfed him.

   He screamed, calling for help, but a darkness so profound absorbed the sound from his lips. Scurrying in the void, he clawed at a wall of curved obsidian. From the emptiness, bone-thin fingers probed at him, caressing, and raking into ripe flesh. He mouthed a silent scream.

Christopher lives in the UK with his wife and daughter. He is currently working on a collection of short stories.

Got Milk? by Mike Murphy

Her littlest sibling would slowly die.

No food for him. No room at the milk-giving teats. She would see to that.

With such a large family vying for places at the "dinner table," Mother wouldn't notice one of her kittens was wasting away until it was too late.

No one cared about the runt of the litter anyway. She would slyly take his meals.

Killing him would be great training for the job she *so* wanted: A witch's familiar. To think that Satan himself might one day gift her to a witch for protection and assistance.

Ah, perchance to dream!

Mike Murphy's tales have been published in audio, prose, and film. See his blog [at audioauthor.blogspot.com] for his credits.

Candle for Knife by Joachim Heijndermans

I light the candle and pray. Pray for not too many folks dying. Pray for Knife to have had enough to cut.

"Please, dear Knife. Please be happy tonight. Don't make me do it again. Let tonight be a good night, where you, dear Knife, don't need the blood on your edge. Please?"

Then I look at my hand, where Knife rests, its handle drenched in my sweat. The light against the blade flickers furiously.

"Go," it whispers. "Make them bleed."

Outside I hear the voices of the people from the street, and I cry, just a little.

Joachim Heijndermans is a writer and artist from the Netherlands. His work is featured in SFFH magazines, podcasts, and animation.

If… by Liam Hogan

If you live long enough, you will attend the funeral of someone you love.

If you live long enough, you will contemplate ending it all.

If you live long enough, you will experience such changes that you will be unable to explain how it was in your day.

If you live long enough, a disaster of world proportions will touch you personally.

If you live long enough, you will doubt everything you thought you knew.

If you live long enough, the ancient one said with a sad shake of her head, you will *not* ask the question you just asked.

Liam Hogan is an award-winning short story writer, published by *Analog*, *Daily Science Fiction*, and *Flame Tree Press*. http://happyendingnotguaranteed.blogspot.co.uk

The Crocodile Promised He'd Eat You Last by Jacob Steven Mohr

It was blood, sticking on her palms and between her fingers. Her parents, her school friends, her beloved pets—they gave up what they had. Now husks rotted in high piles in the basement like spent cocoons. And the knife was clean and back in the block on the kitchen counter. But her hands were still dirty, and dark with blood. It crumbled in the creases, between the pads of a finger and thumb. The big house had never felt colder.

"Please," she begged. "I've given you everything I have."

"No," breathed a reaching, long-fingered voice. "Not everything. Not yet."

Jacob Steven Mohr is a dark fiction author operating out of Columbus OH. His work has appeared in SUMMER BLUDGEON, NIGHT TERRORS, and I CAST YOU OUT!

Siren of the Sand Bar by Dana Vickerson

The rain turned the gravel to slush, but still Elliot pulled the row boat onto the raging water. He had to reach the sand bar. Had to save her.

Black hair lashed around her face as the girl stood against the wind, watching. Calling to him.

His buddies said he was seeing shit every time they went to the levee to get high. *What girl?* they laughed.

He thought they were fucking with him, but as he rowed straight at the girl, a cold tingle of uncertainty dripped down his body.

It made no difference. He rowed all the harder.

Dana's work appears in *Trembling with Fear* and Tales to Terrify and upcoming in *Human Monsters*. She's on Twitter @dmvickerson.

The Count of Three by Cat Voleur

"I love you," he said, who had never loved anyone.

"I love you too," she said, who had loved far too many.

"Together then?" He asked, though he was not prepared to jump.

"Together," she said, stepping up onto the ledge beside him.

"The count of three?" He asked.

She was ready, so with a sad smile she started off their count, rather than answer. "One."

"Two," he replied.

"Three." She pushed him off and watched lovingly as he plummeted toward the rushing waters below. He didn't scream as he fell. That was disappointing. Her other boyfriends had all screamed.

Cat Voleur is a writer of dark fiction and frequent horror journalist. You can find her on Twitter @Cat_Voleur.

What Has Been Given Can Be Taken Away by Stephen Howard

Such a simple mission: find a new home. We both knew our return to Earth was unlikely, but this... this was beyond our comprehension.

Tethered to our shuttle, drifting like flotsam, Clara and I held hands. Her grip tightened.

"Why is it moving towards us?" she whispered, eyes dead ahead.

"Scientifically? I don't know. Spiritually? Maybe God has had enough."

I pulled Clara into me and embraced her. Clara's crucifix, formerly threaded through a loop in her suit, floated past me, loose, lost. The universe's retraction continued, swallowing stars and asteroids and planets and debris. Swallowing the crucifix. Swallowing us.

Stephen Howard is a writer of fantasy, sci-fi, and horror fiction, whose work has been published by *Lost Boys Press, Scribble, Ghost Orchid Press,* and others. You can visit his website https://stephenhowardblog.wordpress.com or find him on Twitter @SteJHoward.

The Last Woman by Sarah Jane Huntington

The woman emerged from the deep pit after twenty-two days.
 Wild thirst and hunger drove her out, that and the smell of rotten corpses.
 Only a wasteland faced her, her vibrant city was no more.
 The sky contained an amber glow, fire, and fury still held in the atmosphere.
 Smoke spiraled and chaos surrounded her. Her lungs burned with poisonous air.
 Her feet crushed the bones of the dead as she stumbled forward.
 War. Bombs.
 Such horrific destruction.
 "Stop."
 She obeyed the voice behind her and dropped to her knees, afraid.
 Soldiers.
 "Please," she begged.
 The bullet killed her instantly.

Sarah Jane Huntington is the author of several short story collections, one novel and one novella. Her work has appeared in many anthologies.

The Dance Demon by Renata Pavrey

Dorian awakes in the evening, stretching out his elastic limbs. The dance demon growls with glee, as the steady drumbeat tickles his pointy ears. Red eyes aglow, he follows the scent of the melody. Now that someone's dancing, Dorian has a body to possess.

He crosses domains dancing in the dark and finds his victim. But wait! *She isn't dancing! Where's the music coming from?*

That vile exorcist played his favorite song to lure the dance demon into this world. This isn't a human body; it's a doll he's inside! Trapped within a plastic toy, the demon dances no more.

Renata Pavrey is a nutritionist, whose writing has appeared in magazines, journals, books and zines. Find her on Twitter @writerlylegacy.

The Trumpet by Will Shadbolt

On a particularly hot July afternoon the angels appeared. They looked like thin, beautiful humans, with osprey-brown, canoe-sized wings sprouting from their backs. One holding a trumpet, later identified as Gabriel, proclaimed, "God was dead," and blew his instrument.

Nothing happened. No lightning. No earthquakes. No storms.

What it signaled was worse.

"Struck Him down myself," Gabriel continued. "The Old bastard kept us all as slaves…"

Their faces began to melt into horns and scabs. Their wings shed their feathers; they were as scaly as a dragon.

"And you'll soon see what he put us through," the demon Gabriel said.

Will Shadbolt works in publishing and lives in Connecticut. You can read more at willshadbolt.com and on Twitter at @W_Shadbolt.

New Life by Clint White

"In the name of the Father..."

He saw the white-robed people scattered across the riverbanks. He gripped the preacher's arm and plunged below the water. Feet planted in shifty sediments. Then he rushed back through the surface.

"And the Son..."

He gasped, his eyes darted, and he was shoved back under. His toes clenched for riverbed sands. As he resurfaced, gulping air, he saw un-peopled banks, empty white robes strewn like carrion.

"And the Holy Ghost..."

Immersed again and there was no riverbed, just water and depth. Around him, his people swam. The preacher's hands held him firmly in place.

Clint White writes weird fiction, lives in Columbus, Ohio, and projects his digital identity on Twitter @clintrwhite

The Sounds of Space and Silence by Jenna Hanchey

Most people spoke to spaceships. Gave them names. Caressed them, cooing gently.

Not Sebastian. He walked his ship's corridors warily, shrinking from both its harsh light and impenetrable darkness.

His ship wanted to kill him.

This truth rang in his ears, increasing in volume. Until it beat like a mad heart. Or war drum.

So Sebastian attacked first.

Clarifying fear lent a rhythm to his blows: Bah-dum. Bah-dum.

Then he ran.

Rounding corners to the escapepod, the pounding levelled into an indistinguishable white noise. As he sprinted.

Slipped.

Fell.

Microseconds before darkness descended, the sound resolved.

The ship was laughing.

Jenna Hanchey's stories appear (or will) in *Nature: Futures, Daily Science Fiction,* and *Martian Magazine*. More at: www.twitter.com/jennahanchey or www.jennahanchey.com.

Cŵn Annwn by Ria Rees

We clamber up the mountain, heaving over rocks, practically crawling. A long, mournful howl carries on the wind.

"Cŵn Annwn," Eleri whispers, "Arawn's hellhounds."

I keep pushing up the steep slope. "We're safe so long as we hear them. Arawn only hunts wrongdoers."

"You've never done anything wrong?" The howls grow quieter.

"Have you?" I look over my shoulder.

She scours the heathers, wide-eyed and panting. "Everyone has."

The mountain is quiet.

My gaze shifts—a massive white hound with red-tipped ears closes in, blood dribbling from its jaws.

I'm speechless, even as it sinks its fangs into her neck.

Ria Rees writes dark scifi and horror in her cosy Welsh cottage, praying her creations will never become sentient. www.riarees.com

Payback by Collin Yeoh

"Please!" sobbed Susan. "Don't do this!"

"Oh, I'm gonna. A bullet in the head's too good for you," said Keisha from behind the barred door.

The zombie was missing an arm below the elbow and most of its guts. What it still had were legs, which it used to shuffle inexorably towards Susan.

"You can probably fight 'im off," said Keisha, grinning. "But not before it bites you."

"But *why*? We're the only two people still alive in this town! *Why are you doing this??*"

Keisha scowled. "Because that's what snitchin' on my weed to the principal *gets* you, *Susan*."

Collin Yeoh enjoys writing horror drabbles. They're so much fun! He lives in Bangkok and misses Malaysian food.

Surprises Suck by Wondra Vanian

Crystal hated surprises.

She'd hated it when her parents tried to surprise her the morning of her sixteenth birthday – only to be the ones surprised when they found her bed empty.

She'd hated it when her friends livestreamed the promposal that had ended in a "Never!" when Jesse Skinner got so nervous he threw up all over her.

And now... *now*.

Here she was, stopped on the way back to her dorm in sweat-drench gym clothes, staring down a crazy guy with a gun, annoyed she had to die smelling like *this*.

Crystal hated surprises. Her murder was no exception.

Wondra Vanian is an American living in the United Kingdom with her Welsh husband and their army of fur babies.

Aberrant Foliation by Dennis Mombauer

The train stopped. Sanesh awoke with a start. His own reflection stared at him from the window. Blackest night reigned outside, and the jungle brushed against the carriage.

"What is going on?" The compartment was abandoned. The ceiling lamps flickered.

Someone knocked on the door, and the metal shuddered. Sanesh turned and foundd his reflection gone, the window just a square of empty darkness.

Another knock.

"Who is there?"

Sanesh inched closer. The handle moved, the door swung open.

As the train accelerated again, Sanesh awoke with a start: and from within the window, he stared at his own reflection.

Dennis Mombauer currently lives in Colombo, Sri Lanka, where he works on climate change and as a writer of speculative fiction and textual experiments. He is co-publisher of a German magazine for experimental fiction, "Die Novelle – Magazine for Experimentalism," and has published fiction and non-fiction in various magazines and anthologies. His English-language debut novella, "The House of Drought," is coming out on July 14th, 2022, with *Stelliform Press*.

Homepage: https://dennismombauer.com/ / Twitter: https://twitter.com/DMombauerWriter

The Coal Ghosts by Abi Marie Palmer

The sightings began before the ashes settled in the mine. Mrs Harris saw her husband's broad figure in the smoke from her burned casserole minutes after his death was confirmed. Next, the slouching silhouette of Johnny Lewis appeared in the cigarette smoke at the pool room. Few believed the stories.

Then, a sudden fire at the house of the proprietor – the one who had declared that work must continue on that fateful day, the one who had ignored the urgent warnings. People believed then. They say the ghosts of the miners danced in the swirling ash as the building burned.

Abi Marie Palmer writes stories inspired by urban legends, folktales and cheesy monster movies. You can find more of her work at abimariepalmer.com

Unholy Choir by James Aitchison

The moon grazes Trastevere's ancient rooftops, spilling shadows along medieval alleyways, some no wider than a child's outstretched arms. The Mad Monk Sistus slips from a ruined church, his hooded robe black as death.

Sistus knows the gravity of sin. Passing beneath a canopy of grapevines, he hears distant voices — his Dead Choir of Rome — praising eternity.

Sistus moves silently, seeking new choir members.

There! A young couple, locked in a shadowy, sinful kiss.

With superhuman strength, the Mad Monk strangles them both with the cord of his robe, carrying them back to his crypt where they will sing forever.

Australian author James Aitchison writes horror as Mike Rader. His stories have appeared via *Horror Tree, Black Hare Press,* and more.

Torches, Pitchforks by Jacob Steven Mohr

The castle gates fall like great timber; the woman scurries down four winding flights, into darkness, then into antiseptic laboratory light. Her white coat beats the air like a wing until she slams the heavy bolt closed and slumps against the door, listening to the blood rush in her ears.

The mob thunders down towards her; she draws a pistol and pulls the hammer back. Across the room—a half-complete corpse lays stiff on its slab, cold flesh peppered with electrodes. Its eyes follow her with no expression.

"I'm sorry," she whispers to it, nosing the barrel under her chin.

Jacob Steven Mohr is a dark fiction author operating out of Columbus OH. His work has appeared in SUMMER BLUDGEON, NIGHT TERRORS, and I CAST YOU OUT!

Hurricane Warning by Alex Luceli Jiménez

Sometimes you're in the headlines after I help you bury a body, but never your name. I'm the only one who knows it's you. You've taught me how the world doesn't make sense: you, a killer, hiding even the butter knives so I can't hurt myself. But I've loved you since we were two little girls riding bikes in our small town, so I help you bury bodies. In our city apartment we sleep in silk nightgowns and you sing me to sleep. The blood has been washed off your hands. Still I see red when I look at you.

Alex Luceli Jiménez is a queer Mexican writer and middle school English teacher living in Soledad, CA. Her writing has appeared or is forthcoming in Berkeley Fiction Review, Barren Magazine, Ram Eye Press, and Tales From Between. She was born and raised in southern California. Visit her online at alexlucelijimenez.com and on Twitter @alexluceli.

Way Up High by Rachel L. Tilley

I don't know how I wound up unconscious, only that I woke to discover myself tied to the peak of a redwood tree – the victim of a cruel joke. Someone was mocking my fear of heights.

I dare not tug the bindings; to test the strength of my restraints.

Then I notice them – beryl eyes, glowing against the night sky. Faint moonlight glinting off protracted claws.

Raw-boned creatures are shambling up the trunk towards me, saliva dripping from their feral mouths. An ear-piercing keening resounds.

I try to untie myself; I'd rather jump.

But the shackles are secure after all.

Rachel L. Tilley, who lives in the UK, writes short stories in the fantasy and horror genres.

www.instagram.com/rachel_l_tilley

Snow Day by Bethany Browning

The bomb cyclone had trapped our parents at a ski resort and us at home with our babysitter.

Gorgas was a widow from church who smelled like ammonia and yeast. We'd gone feral from five days of sugary snacks, giggle fits, and sibling scuffles.

"There's something on the porch," we said. "We're scared," we said. Gorgas squinted. The door creaked as she opened it. She stepped out. "Here?" she asked. "A little bit farther," we said.

I snapped the lock. We turned up the TV to drown out her begging. Gorgas went silent, and we argued over what to watch.

Bethany Browning writes horror, mystery and dark humor. Find links to her published work at bethanybrowning.com.

The Motes by Tess P.

The Motes, flutter and fly. Particles of humans that once walked this house; absorbing your feelings and fears, delight and disgust. You lay there in sodden sheets with guilt ridden angst of an ill led life. A shaft of dawn breaks through the half shut drapes. Your red rimmed eyes watch the Motes as they dance in their knowing way; mocking your madness, your shame, your selfish smile. They have seen it: the sickening debauchery you dragged into this room. So, now they wait, hanging above your head; knowing you will soon join them. Ashes to ashes, dust to dust.

Tess pens horror shorts and dark drabbles. You'll find her on Twitter @Tess_2020 engaging within the writing community.

Predators and Prey by Taylor Rae

The zookeeper returns too soon.

His showman-laugh echoes down the hall. He's brought visitors.

He doesn't feed you enough, but that might save you. Your bone-thin hands can finally slip through the cage bars. Your hairpin click-clicks in the lock.

"The final exhibit," he says, "is my career highlight."

They're appraising the other girls he hunted. His human zoo.

Click-click.

The visitors coyote-cackle with him. Men's laughter terrifies you now.

Click-click. The lock gives.

You emerge with a tin shard, sharpened into a blade.

But you don't run.

You crouch, hidden, waiting.

You'll show him the fear of being hunted.

Taylor Rae's work has appeared with *Flash Fiction Online, NYC Midnight,* and *Pseudopod.* For more, check out www.mostlytaylor.com

Welcome to the Funhouse by Alicia Hilton

The funhouse clown had really long fangs and a loud, annoying laugh, but Daisy and Tricia walked through his mouth anyway.

The skeleton in the first room wasn't very scary, even when his left arm fell off with a *clatter*.

Rubber spiders and skittering roaches made Tricia squeal and run for the exit.

Daisy stopped in front of the wobbly mirror and looked at her reflection.

The girl in the mirror wore jeans and a plaid shirt like Daisy, but her eyes were stitched closed and blood dripped down her face. She said, "Wish you were here," and grabbed Daisy.

Alicia Hilton's stories have appeared in *Daily Science Fiction, Vastarien,* and *Year's Best Hardcore Horror.* Her website is https://aliciahilton.com.

Publication History

A Scorching Mother by Ai Jiang is original to this anthology.

The Mess You've Made by Taylor Rae was originally published in Lulu.com's 2020 *Share Your Scare Vol. 4*.

Inside by Michelle Ann King was originally published in *Postcard Shorts* (Jan 2012)

Beside a Cemetery, a Stone Wall, a Skeletal Tree by Elou Carroll is original to this anthology.

In the Wee Hours by Dorian J. Sinnott is original to this anthology.

Emma by Dorian J. Sinnott is original to this anthology.

After Glow by Liam Hogan was originally published in *Black Hare Press*'s "Dark Moments" series, July 2019.

By the Coin by Stace Johnson is original to this anthology.

Ephemeral by Antony Frost is original to this anthology.

Playing in the Woods by Carson Winter is original to this anthology.

The Creative Writing Assignment by TJ Price is original to this anthology.

The Scarecrow Sang to Empty Rows of Silage by Mathew Wend is original to this anthology.

Hatman by Chelsea Pumpkins is original to this anthology.

The Quiet Things in Forgotten Spaces by Jessica Peter is original to this anthology.

Cracking Porcelain by Vanessa Jae is original to this anthology.

Light Switch Serenade by Nikki R. Leigh is original to this anthology.

Interior Monologue by John H. Dromey is original to this anthology.

The Drowned Witches of the Ashen Sea by Tea Riffo is original to this anthology.

Post-Apocalyptic Saturday by Patrick Barb is original to this anthology.

Down By The Reef by Grant Butler is original to this anthology.

Cù-Sìth by Emma Louise Gill is original to this anthology.

In the Boneyard Good by Joachim Heijndermans is original to this anthology.

Waiting for a Whisper by Dana Vickerson is original to this anthology.

Mom Swears This Will Work by Tyler Norton is original to this anthology.

The Last Fantasy by Warren Benedetto is original to this anthology.

Everything You Know About Witches by Warren Benedetto was originally published in *Dark Moments* by Black Hare Press (October 2020).

PUBLICATION HISTORY

Small Mercies by Mob is original to this anthology.

Merdreams by Stephanie Parent was originally published in *The Drabble*.

Before the Storm by Stephanie Parent is original to this anthology.

Rubin's Vase is Rife With Larvae by Bob McHugh is original to this anthology.

The Hungry by C.M. Saunders is original to this anthology.

Code Blue by NJ Gallegos is original to this anthology.

A Hunger for Company by Kai Delmas is original to this anthology.

Cabbage Dismemberment by Joshua Herz is original to this anthology.

The Bridge Game by Marc Sorondo is original to this anthology.

Knife by Kailey Alessi is original to this anthology.

The Angels by Will Shadbolt is original to this anthology.

The Hunt by Liam Hogan is original to this anthology.

The Outage on Burberry Lane by Dorian J. Sinnott is original to this anthology.

The Horsemen by Cody Simpson is original to this anthology.

The Angel by Warren Benedetto was originally published in *Infection* by Black Ink Fiction in June 2021.

Voices by Kailey Alessi is original to this anthology.

The Wish in the Woods by Abigail Winslow is original to this anthology.

They Came From the Deep by Joe Scipione is original to this anthology.

Life Sentence by M. L. Grieve is original to this anthology.

A Sleeping Sickness by Belicia Rhea is original to this anthology.

The Sommelier by Tess P. is original to this anthology.

Simulation by Andrea Allison was originally published in *Trembling With Fear* and *Trembling With Fear: Year 3* Anthology.

Mama by T.L. Beeding is original to this anthology.

Runaway Wood by Ian Kitley is original to this anthology.

Someone to Love by R.A. Goli is original to this anthology.

Trail of Slime by DJ Tyrer was originally published in *Japanese Fantasy Drabbles* (Insignia Stories, 2020).

A Lidded Black Box by Christopher Wood is original to this anthology.

Got Milk? by Mike Murphy is original to this anthology.

Candle for Knife by Joachim Heijndermans is original to this anthology.

If… by Liam Hogan is original to this anthology.

The Crocodile Promised He'd Eat You Last by Jacob Steven Mohr is original to this anthology.

PUBLICATION HISTORY

Siren of the Sand Bar by Dana Vickerson is original to this anthology.

The Count of Three by Cat Voleur was originally published in *HorrorAddicts* in 2017.

What Has Been Given Can Be Taken Away by Stephen Howard is original to this anthology.

The Last Woman by Sarah Jane Huntington is original to this anthology.

The Dance Demon by Renata Pavrey was originally published in *Forest of Fear* by Blood Song Books.

The Trumpet by Will Shadbolt was originally published in *ANGELS: A Divine Microfiction Anthology* by Black Hare Press in 2019.

New Life by Clint White is original to this anthology.

The Sounds of Space and Silence by Jenna Hanchey is original to this anthology.

Cŵn Annwn by Ria Rees is original to this anthology.

Payback by Collin Yeoh is original to this anthology.

Surprises Suck by Wondra Vanian is original to this anthology.

Aberrant Foliation by Dennis Mombauer was originally published in *Dark Moments* by Black Hare Press in 2019.

The Coal Ghosts by Abi Marie Palmer is original to this anthology.

Unholy Choir by James Aitchison is original to this anthology.

Torches, Pitchforks by Jacob Steven Mohr is original to this anthology.

Hurricane Warning by Alex Luceli Jiménez is original to this anthology.

Way Up High by Rachel L. Tilley is original to this anthology.

Snow Day by Bethany Browning is original to this anthology.

The Motes by Tess P. is original to this anthology.

Predators and Prey by Taylor Rae was originally published in Lulu.com's 2020 *Share Your Scare Vol. 4*.

Welcome to the Funhouse by Alicia Hilton was originally published in *Stupefying Stories*.

Also by Shacklebound Books

I hope you enjoyed Drabbledark II: An Anthology of Dark Drabbles. There are many more drabble anthologies by Shacklebound Books and I hope you'll check those out too. You can also follow Shacklebound Books' newsletter for a free story every month, a book deal, new releases, and submission calls for writers.

Sign up here: http://eepurl.com/hVYX9j

Drabbledark: An Anthology of Dark Drabbles
Drabbledark: An Anthology of Dark Drabbles is an anthology of drabbles, stories of exactly 100 words in length. Within these pages are 101 tales of dark fantasy, horror, and science fiction from 86 new and veteran voices of speculative fiction. This anthology combines both original fiction and reprints, with a majority of original fiction, celebrating the power of micro flash fiction in the form of dark plots and themes.

Chronos: An Anthology of Time Drabbles
Chronos is an anthology of drabbles (a story told in exactly one-hundred words) themed around time. Seventy-five talented authors from around the world come together to present ninety-eight stories of time, time travel, time zones, time manipulation, flash-forwards, space-time, time freezes, and so many other variations on the theme.

Martian Year One

Martian is a magazine of science fiction drabbles, stories told in exactly 100 words. This is the complete first year of Martian, containing all four of our first issues. This anthology features stories from Rich Larson, D.A. Xiaolin Spires, Lora Gray, Lettie Prell, Steve Rasnic Tem, Holly Schofield, Wendy Nikel, Liam Hogan, and many other writers from around the globe.

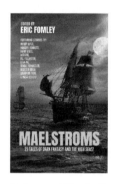

Maelstroms: 23 Tales of Dark Fantasy and the High Seas!

Maelstroms is an anthology of dark fantasy flash fiction stories set on or around the high seas. Within these pages are pirates, mermaids, the Kraken, storms, haunted places, creepy creatures, and many other dark imaginings from authors Wendy Nikel, Dorian J. Sinnott, Dawn Vogel, Ai Jiang, Lena NG, Dennis Mombauer, Rebecca Birch, Jonathan Ficke, and 15 others!

Made in the USA
Middletown, DE
01 September 2024